S0-BNY-469

Black Cocktail

BY THE SAME AUTHOR

The Land of Laughs
Voice of Our Shadow
Bones of the Moon
Sleeping in Flame
A Child Across the Sky
Die Panische Hand
Outside the Dog Museum

BLACK COCKTAIL

Jonathan Carroll

Illustrated by Dave McKean

St. Martin's Press
New York

BLACK COCKTAIL. Copyright © 1990 by Jonathan Carroll. Illustrations ©
1990 by Dave McKean. All rights reserved. Printed in the United States of
America. No part of this book may be used or reproduced in any manner
whatsoever without written permission except in the case of brief quotations
embodied in critical articles or reviews. For information, address St. Martin's
Press, 175 Fifth Avenue, New York, N.Y. 10010.

Library of Congress Cataloging-in-Publication Data

Carroll, Jonathan.
    Black cocktail / Jonathan Carroll.
        p.   cm.
    ISBN 0-312-06304-0
    I. Title.
    PS3553.A7646B57   1991
    813′.54—dc   91-19052
                                                          CIP

First published in Great Britain by Random Century Group.

First U.S. Edition: September 1991
10 9 8 7 6 5 4 3 2 1

Whatever tastiness or bite this cocktail might have is due in large part to the intuition and expertise of my editor, Deborah Beale. *Mon chapeau* –

For Diane Wakoski

Black Cocktail

One of the things I loved about Michael Billa from the very beginning was his stories. There are some people who have the glorious ability to take the smallest, most forgettable events and transform them in the telling into adventures, a slice across the heart – or, at the very least, a good healthy laugh that dusts off the old boring shelves of our days.

'I had a telephone number once that was only one digit different from a city employment office. People were constantly calling and asking for a Mr Posamenti, Director of Municipal Employment. I'd be very nice and say sorry, wrong number. But after about the fiftieth time, my eyes crossed and I started seeing red.

'Another thing that drove me nuts was how stupid some of these callers were. Half of them sounded like they'd had trouble figuring out how to dial the phone! And hearing they'd made a mistake, I could tell some were really *suspicious* and thought I was trying to fool them . . . This was the right number, but I was just a nasty little creep trying to trick 'em!

'One morning the phone rang when I was in a pissy mood. When the guy said "I'd like to speak with Mr Posamenti", I stopped a moment, looked at the phone, and said "This is he."

' "Well, my name is Rickie Otto and I'd like to have a job with the city."

' "What are your qualifications, Mr Otto?"

' "Waddya mean?"

' "What kind of work have you done previously to deserve a job with the city?"

' "I'm a Veteran and I've driven a truck. I'll take a job driving a truck for the city."

' "That sounds good enough. Why don't we make an appointment right now?"

' "Okay by me."

' "Good, Mr Otto. Then I'd like you to come down to the Municipal Building next Tuesday morning, office number 32, dressed as an owl. Will that be convenient?"

' "Dressed as a *what*? What'd you say?"

' "Dressed as an owl, Mr Otto." '

Michael also smokes wonderfully. He knows how to take the most dramatic drag on a cigarette and time it so that, while he's inhaling, whatever he's just said is sinking down inside you so it hits bottom and explodes just as he's about to speak again.

He smiled and shrugged, blew smoke towards the ceiling. 'Otto didn't say anything for the *longest* time, then just hung up. Click.'

We met in a mysterious, romantic way.

Glenn, the man I had been living with, was killed in that terrible earthquake that did such damage to Los Angeles recently. We were very much in love and had remained true to each other. We considered ourselves two of the lucky ones in these Plague Days of AIDS, when so many of our other gay friends had either died of the disease or were waiting for their blood test results with little hope. Glenn had often bitterly joked that gays had gone from being social to physical pariahs in less than one generation. But the two of us had somehow come out of it all right: we had our love, we had our health, we both had jobs many people envied.

Then one evening when Glenn was out on the patio, the earthquake struck. Our house was literally split in half by the force of the quake and came down in giant pieces on top of my friend.

I was driving home from the radio station. Miraculously the only thing I felt was a cartoonishly strong buckling and rolling on the freeway, a scene straight out of a Mickey Mouse dream. I remember the grey and black pavement undulating like an eel, flipping cars and trucks in the air as if they were weightless. All the hours it took to get home afterwards, I couldn't stop thinking about how afraid of earthquakes Glenn was; how often he'd said we had to move out of the state before the big one came. Smiling, I'd say, 'How can you move out of California when you're so successful?'

He'd say, 'Because you can't be successful when you're dead, Ingram.'

That's what I thought about while crossing the split and groaning face of Los Angeles that night of loss. Although it is very beautiful in the winter in LA, it gets dark fast. By the time I got to our house, it was around eight and black. Almost all of the lights were off everywhere, no cars moved on the badly broken street, the only sounds the sharp close crackle and hiss of fires, sirens, helicopters whopping low in the air every few minutes.

When I realised I was standing in front of where I'd lived that morning, I flung myself onto what was left and began to dig.

There's a whole other story there, but it isn't what I started out to talk about. Besides, I am not as good a storyteller as Michael, so all you would get from me on this are more tears and pleas to the dead and the living to understand why I wasn't able to save the life of the man I loved.

We found Glenn before he died. Yes, somehow found him in that stink of stone and smoke. Working with our next-door neighbour, I pulled what was left of him out of the pile. Only to watch him let go of my hand, try to smile, die.

11

After he was buried (remember all the new cemeteries that sprang up after that, with places like Forest Lawn in such chaos? Real estate prices once again soared in California, only this time for space below, rather than above, ground), I wrote my sister Maris a letter about it. Two surprising things resulted: I received her reply very quickly, which, considering the state of things in California post-quake, was remarkable. Secondly, in her letter she told me to call a man named Michael Billa. Her husband suggested I get in touch with Billa because he knew the two of us would 'get along'. Only that.

I'd met my sister's husband a few times and although I liked him, I was put off by his presumptuousness here: how could he begin to *think* he knew the kind of person I'd 'get along' with?

But loneliness takes no prisoners; it either kills you or leaves you alone. It almost killed me. After sifting the rubble of the earthquake and my life, I found I wanted to save so little. A handful of things (besides memories) to brush off, have repaired, *keep* . . .

Shortly after that, there was a time when I browsed at the windows of gun stores, and made lists of doctors I knew who might be willing to write me strange prescriptions.

That passed, but a feeling of sad weightlessness didn't. Death has various courses on its menu besides the old solid-line stop of brain waves, or the heart's reliable thump.

In fact it was Michael who said death was like a bartender who can whip up any number of exotic drinks, besides the standard beer-and-a-shot, or double vodka.

'Think of the varieties of death, Ingram. I grew up in a town full of old Sicilian women. Many of their husbands had been dead since they were very young, but when that happened, *sixty* years ago, these dames

12

put on black mourning clothes and *pffft*! Whatever sexy or alive stuff they had in them just gave up the ghost along with the husbands. And remember, these women were eighteen when it happened, eighty when I knew them!

'Or in school I knew this guy who didn't get into Yale ... Something died in the son of a bitch the moment that happened! I'm telling you, to this day he's never stopped talking about how he got fucked by the Yale Admission Committee. This is a man who has been very successful in life! Whatever it was – his high school ego, an assurance he had until the day that letter came from Yale – RIP, Rest In Peace.

'Small deaths. Deaths we can afford because we have so much else that goes on living in us. A drink analogy works there too – some people drink and drink, knowing they're getting looped. But usually they can afford to "lose" some qualities, let them die for the day, because of the situation. I'm not driving tonight? Then I don't have to see so straight. We're with friends? Then I can be an ass.'

'You think wearing a lampshade on your head is a kind of death?'

'Sure, the death of good sense. Dangerous stuff, if the wrong people find out. You know that. Look at the weirdos on your show.'

I'm a radio talk-show host. For the past five years I have run a hot potato called *Off the Wall* which welcomes full-blown kooks to come in, have a seat, and get whatever they want off their quivering chests. The show is strange, popular, and more often than one'd suppose, startling. The people who come on are creative as well as (usually) crazy. Doing the show reminds me of Mark Twain's line about wanting to go to Hell, rather than Heaven, because that's where all the interesting people are. Whatever one thinks about *Off the Wall*, it's an interesting hour in your ear.

Once in a while the genuine article comes on – a mystic who really does have a profound and intimate vision of life's mysteries, or a fortune teller who takes one look and says three things about you you didn't want to hear. But they are rare, and the rest of my guests are dangling high tension wires of energy, plots, messages, secrets from the beyond.

The show is a success because I like interviewing these people, like hearing their stories and whatever else they have to say. Someone once asked Ronald Reagan why he thought he was so popular with the American people. He said it was because people sensed he genuinely liked them. That's how I feel about the folks who come to *Off the Wall*. I like them and want to hear their stories.

The only thing that kept me even partially afloat after Glenn's death was the show. Mad or not, the guests are invariably charged with a special kind of energy when they walk through the studio doors, here to sell turtle ranches on Pluto or talk about the Omelette People who inhabit their backyard. But what often pulled me through to another day was realizing, through the show, how exhilarating and varied life is. Things may be pretty damned shitty for you right now, but in the next moment or hour they will be interesting or at least changing. All I had to do was look at the list of visitors on the show and I'd know that if there was a man who lived underneath a horse, or a woman who believed her clock was Elvis Presley, then there had to be other places for me, other possibilities, another man who would say 'Yes, come here: we have things to talk about.'

So I didn't buy a gun and I didn't take pills, but, one night when I realized I'd been looking at my hands for too long a time, I *did* get out my address book and call the man my brother-in-law thought I'd get along with.

15

Why the hell not?

Michael was hesitant at first, but I heard a curiosity in his voice as well that said he'd be willing to take one tentative step in my direction if I didn't move too quickly and 'flush' him like a bird when it stands in front of you.

'Do you like a good hot fudge sundae?'

'You're talking my language.'

'Let's meet at C. C. Brown's on Hollywood Boulevard.'

I tape *Off the Wall* early in the afternoon two days a week so I can have those evenings free. The night I walked into the ice cream parlour, ironically the last thing I heard on the street before going through the door was the beginning of Cabaret Voltaire's eerie funk song 'Sensoria' coming from someone's car: the theme song to *Off the Wall*. I didn't know if that was a good or bad omen.

There were two men sitting alone in booths. One was half-hidden behind a newspaper, the other looked at the door while running a finger inside the collar of his shirt. The man behind the paper looked fat, the other playing with his collar too nervous. Neither looked promising.

'Hey, Ingram York!'

The greeting came from behind. The voice sounded very familiar. As I turned to meet Michael Billa, I saw Willy Snakespeare instead. Willy was a regular on my show and would come on at a moment's notice when we needed a chatty 'character' to liven things up. He was funny, could talk about all kinds of things, and was crazy as they get. He lived with two boa constrictors named Laverne and Surly that he'd bring to the studio whenever he came. I liked Willy, in small doses, but didn't need him that night. Billa knew what I did for a living, but at our first meeting I didn't want

16

living scary proof of the kind of people I voluntarily surrounded myself with daily.

'I would've brought the snakes with me if I'd known I was going to bump into you!'

'Hiya, Willy. I'll see ya, Willy.'

'How 'bout an ice cream, Ingram? I just got my pension cheque and want to treat you to an ice cream.'

'Thanks, Willy, but I'm meeting someone here. Can I have a rain-check on it?'

He looked at me the way a duck looks at you – to the side and with full attention. 'I-smell-smoke! You got a date waiting, huh?'

'A friend.'

He smiled. 'You ever hear the story about Jack Nicholson? He was at a party where this beautiful woman walks up to him and says "Hiya, Jack, wanna dance?" Jack gives her the once-over and says, "Wrong verb, honey. You're using the wrong verb!" '

Willy told the story loudly. When he finished, someone behind us laughed loud and appreciatively. I turned and saw the fat man, newspaper down, his face wrinkled in a big smile. Maybe he wasn't fat – just big, large everything. A weightlifter, or a one-time football player? When he looked at me he waved and gestured to come over. Willy patted my back and walked out.

Michael half-rose from his seat and put out a giant hand to shake.

'You're so big. You sound mid-size on the phone.'

'Speaking of voices, say "Hello. The Aliens Have Landed." '

I was surprised. 'You listen to my show?'

'Sometimes. It's a little rich for my blood, but I like the way you handle it; you treat the people like they're real and not rare tropical fish.'

I sat down. 'Some of them *are* tropical fish. They just grow legs so they can walk to the show.

17

'When I came in before, I didn't know which one was you.'

He turned palms up. 'I always forget to tell people to look for the big guy. I'm not hard to find if I say that.

'But I'll tell you something – I forget I'm tall. When I was a kid, we had a golden retriever that must have weighed eighty pounds. Big damned dog. But *she* was convinced she was as delicate and petite as a French woman. She'd wrestle her way onto the smallest chair in the house and lie there uncomfortably, pretending the seat suited her fine when it was obvious she needed to be stretched out on the couch. That's me. I buy shoes that pinch my feet, can't believe it when they tell me I'm a fifty-six long suit . . . In my heart I'm Edith Piaf.'

The sundaes came and I told him about working on the show and some of its more colourful characters. He was a fidgety man, but despite playing with silverware or pushing his water glass back and forth across the table, there was no doubt he gave you his full attention.

When it came time to talk about himself, the fidgeting stopped and everything about Michael Billa sort of slowed to a chat-by-the-fire pace. He had things to say and knew you were going to like them and want more, but you had to fix your pace to his and not show impatience. At first I thought it a rude mannerism – giving you the feeling he couldn't wait for you to finish so he could say *his* piece. But after being with him a while, I realized Michael did everything impatiently *but* talk. He had no other hobbies. Talk was his fishing, his stamp collecting, the great long meal at an expensive restaurant with friends. It was the only thing that allowed him to relax.

He ran a successful men's store downtown, 'The Cabinet of Doctor Caligari', and spent most of his time working. He drove a compact car, lived in a well-furnished but small house in Larchmont, and didn't seem to do anything in his spare time besides read.

We ended the evening at a golf driving range in West Hollywood. I hadn't driven golf balls since junior high school, but like bowling or roller skating, it was a gas to go back to something so thoroughly *then* and look at it over your shoulder as if it were a passenger in the back seat of your car.

Michael took off his jacket after smacking the first few balls. He was even bigger than I'd originally thought.

'Did you play football?'

He shook his head. 'People always ask me that, but I didn't. I've never been a good athlete, but I enjoy doing things like this. As a kid I was just fat. You know, the kind who has three candy bars in his lunch bag, then goes home after school and eats a big piece of chocolate cake? God, I was a mess.

'As a kid you want so to be loved, but then you do just about everything possible to make yourself unlovable. Eat too much, take too few baths, whine . . .' He tee'd off on a ball that sailed up across the distance. 'Thank God for Clinton.'

'Who's Clinton?'

He looked at me as if I'd asked a very personal question. There was a pause while he held the golf club just off the ground, twitching it back and forth.

'A kid who saved my life. More than once.'

The bar at the Westwood Muse Hotel is a favourite hang-out of Los Angeles radio people. I suggested it after the driving range. Michael smiled and said he didn't drink but liked a good bar.

'How come, if you don't drink?' I was thinking of his nervousness, his already noticeable inability to sit still for more than a few minutes. A good bar doesn't come to you for at least an hour: you have to relax into

19

it, let it take your hand and show you its best features – its clientele, the music, where it's most cosy.

'Because a good bar is where you're comfortable enough to tell a good story. Even when it takes hours.' Michael was drinking a large glass of ginger ale and grenadine.

We were sitting in the corner by that tank full of blue fish watching a man and wife enter the room. He was very solicitous, but she, a spectacular redhead, looked like the wrath of God. I mentioned that to Michael, who nodded.

'I was just thinking that! She looks as if he's just told her there's another woman.

'One of the most important women in my life had red hair. Eddie Devon; the first woman I ever fantasized about. At fifteen, she had a body that would have sent monks howling. Eddie Devon even chewed gum sexily! Ever noticed how teenage girls chew gum like they've got a mouth *full* of dirty, pink and erotic? The colour of this drink.' He held up his glass. 'Everyone in our school watched her and she knew it. There's a pride in young women that makes them glow – they know they're the centre of attention and the world cares. Maybe down deep they also know it won't last more than a few years, so they revel in it while they can.

'Whatever, Eddie drove us all nuts, including fat guy Mike Billa. You know what it's like being called "Lard Ass" in front of an Eddie Devon? The worst, Ingram. It's got to be one of the mortal wounds of childhood. But we're tough then; so long as I could feel her breezes, then I put up with insults from the other kids. Once in a while she'd even say something nice to me, or smile, which cancelled out a good chunk of the pain.

'God, how long has it been since I thought of that girl? Probably because you reminded me of Clinton before.'

Michael took a long pull on his drink and clunked

it back down on the table with a smile. 'I have to tell you a Clinton and Eddie story.

'His name was Clinton Deix.' (Michael pronounced the surname 'Dikes'.) 'He lived down the street from me in Saint Deborah's Home for Orphans. All the kids who lived at St Deb's were tough, but Clinton was there about five minutes before he'd kicked every bad ass in the place and become boss. Know what he called himself? "The Prince of Fingers and Toes". Don't ask me why. He came from New York, but I never got the details straight about how he'd ended up in St Deborah's, except he told me his parents were dead.

'He was very, very crazy. Probably schizophrenic, but we didn't know big words like that then, so we just thought he had a lot of bad moods. Clinton was the kind of crazy where if he got into a fight, he'd pick up whatever was nearest and bash the guy on the head with it. I saw him do it. A lot of kids in my town were tough, but they knew trouble when they saw it. Clinton was crazy as a fly in a jar.'

'What a strange image. You were friends? I thought you said you were a loser.'

Michael nodded and closed his eyes. 'I was, but you know how some kids pick up on each other for no reason other than strange chemistry? Basically from the day we met, Clinton and I were buddies. The orphanage was right down the street from my house; ten minutes away. We walked home from school together his first day because we found ourselves going in the same direction. When we got to my house he patted my shoulder and said he would see me tomorrow. The next morning he was waiting outside my gate, so we walked together and that was that.

'At lunchtime that second day, Anthony Fanelli called him a "Nazi" and Clinton stuffed a sandwich in Anthony's ear. Egg salad. To this day I can remember that yellow and white glop oozing down the side of

Fanelli's head.' Billa hunched forward and put his hands together excitedly. 'You see, Anthony was tough, but when Clinton stabbed him with the sandwich, it was so fast and violent Fanelli got that scared look in his eye, like maybe I don't want to put my spoon in *this* pot, thank you very much.'

Billa told the story with such relish and remembered glee that I could clearly imagine Fanelli's expression; the shock at being instantly beaten, the shame of knowing you're about to back down in front of *everyone*.

'What'd Fanelli do?'

'Looked straight ahead and ate the other half of his sandwich. Then Eddie Devon walked by with her crowd and stopped to look at him. She made sure people were listening, and said in a bitchy voice, "You've got egg on your face, Anthony."

'Out of the corner of my eye, I saw Clinton hold up his hand and snap his fingers for her attention. We all looked at him because the deal was between them now, although she didn't know it yet: the Queen of school vs. the Prince of Fingers and Toes.

'She looked at him. Clinton reached over and stuck his finger in the egg salad that was still on Anthony's face. When he had a big gob of the stuff, he put it in his mouth and said to Eddie, "It tastes like you." '

Michael and I began hanging around together. Although he often talked too much, I still enjoyed being with him. His greatest qualities were an unconscious kindness and optimism that both awed and shamed me. Before meeting him, I'd thought of myself as a generally decent, fair person who was willing to give where it was needed and not be too quick to judge others. But Michael saw things so sunnily that it was rare when he 'judged' at all; he liked the meals life cooked for him, so he ate them with few complaints and the big appetite of a hungry kid. He was one of the only adults I knew who was genuinely happy with his life, notwithstanding the normal ups and downs we all go through from Monday to Sunday. Being around him was helpful, even inspiring at times. When I told him that, he readily agreed.

'It was my childhood. I'm sure it has to do with that. See, I told you I was your proverbial fat boy who wants the whole world to love him. The thing was, once Clinton Deix came into my life, the world *did* love me. At least, my world did. It was a combination of two things – since Clinton liked me, they had to like me or he'd punch them out. But then this mystique grew up around me. Kids began thinking, well, Mike Billa *must* have something going for him if *Clinton* likes him *so* much, i.e., Billa has some invisible cool we haven't noticed yet, but we will.

'It was one of the greatest "The Emperor's New Clothes" jobs I've ever seen, Ingram. Because I had no cool whatsoever. I was a fatso who got Cs and dreamt of being in with the "In" crowd. Remember that song by Dobie Gray? I thought that was the grooviest thing I ever heard. But what jerk gets to be in with the In crowd? If it hadn't been for Clinton, all of my childhood would have stunk. As it was, he made the years from about twelve on heavenly.'

'Sounds like he was your guardian angel.'

'Without a doubt.'

'What happened to him? Do you ever see him?'

'Now and then.'

We ate Mexican food, went to the beach, argued comfortably about films. About two months after we met, I had one of those epiphanal moments when I realized I'd never love Michael, but that I already did love a number of things about him.

Sex was not part of our relationship. In my mind I was still Glenn's lover and had no wish to break out

24

of that bubble to look for something new. Michael made no move in this direction and I assumed he was either taking things very slow or didn't want our friendship to go that way either.

'When did you first know you were gay?'

We were having lunch at the Gingham Garden restaurant in Larchmont. The sun lit the cloth roof over the terrace and people all around us talked too loudly about their lovers, bad film deals, or illness. Those are the most popular topics of conversation in the film capital of the world, and not always in that order.

I asked the question quietly, but Michael answered like a trumpet fanfare. 'About a year after I met Clinton. He'd stolen some *Playboy*s from the candy store and we were looking at them in my room. He asked if I liked the pictures. I shrugged and said they were all right. He asked if I'd like to screw one of those girls and I said, sure, wouldn't you?

' "Naah. Who'd want to get lost in all that?"

'I didn't know what "all that" was, but it sounded impressive, so I kept quiet. Clinton pulled another magazine out from beneath his shirt and dropped it in front of me as if it were proof of something. Remember in the old days when they wouldn't show frontal nudity in a skin mag? The only place where you could see that was in a nudist magazine like *Sun and Fun* or *Sun Worship*. They cost *three* bucks, which was a fortune then, and pretended to be for "serious nudists".' Michael said the term so loudly that a number of the women around us stopped drinking iced tea and gave him still, freezing stares. He paid no attention.

'Anyway, Clinton put one of those in front of me and then flipped it open to a page of naked men playing volleyball. They looked great – all tight muscle tone and health. And they *did* look better than the girls, who just seemed sort of lost and friendly with their big breasts and magazine smiles. It was the first time I'd

25

seen a woman square-on, but the men were more intriguing and provocative. The women were mysterious and impressive; the men you wanted to reach through the magazine and touch.'

'Did anything happen between you two that day?'

'No. Not then.'

'Later?'

He didn't answer the question because someone he knew came to our table and said hello.

One night on *Off the Wall* I had a bunch of people who said they were the incarnations of famous people. Hitler was there, Mozart, Jean-Jacques Rousseau. The last fifteen minutes of the show were always given over to call-ins from listeners. Hitler had gotten most of the calls (and flak), but someone asked Mozart if he'd liked the film *Amadeus* and if Salieri really had murdered him. Poor Rousseau (a mailman from Tempe, Arizona) was ignored until the last call of the night.

I didn't recognize the voice. 'Mr Rousseau, could you tell me precisely what you meant when you said in Book Six of your *Confessions*: "Believers in general create God in their own image. The good make him good, the evil, evil; fanatics, being full of hatred and bile, can see only hell, because they wish to damn the whole world, while gentle, loving souls hardly believe in such a place." '

Rousseau thought about it a moment, then pulled up close to the microphone. 'God is in the eye of the beholder. A good man sees God as a positive force, the bad man sees Him as a threat. Nothing could be simpler.'

My engineer pointed to the clock. There were only two minutes left and I still had to announce who'd be on the show the next day.

Before I had a chance to say anything, the voice on the telephone said 'Mr Rousseau, don't you think if

26

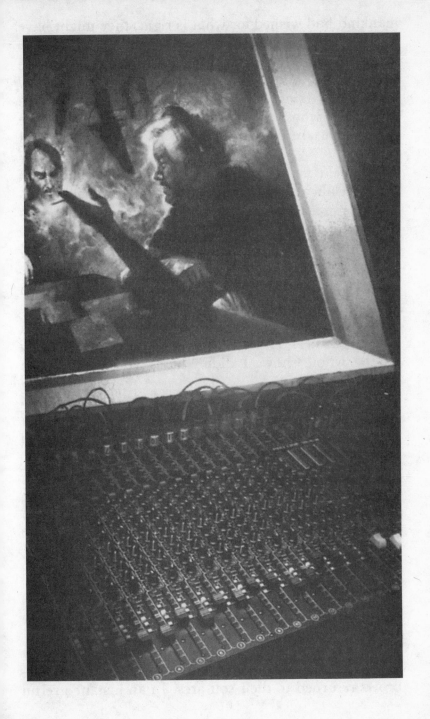

mankind had wished for what is right, they might have had it a long time ago?'

'Sorry, but Mr Rousseau can't answer that because we are plain out of time. Tomorrow on *Off the Wall* we'll be talking to the rock group "Rattlesnake Orgasm" whose only instruments are microwave ovens. You are cordially invited to join us. Over and out!'

The next morning I drove over to 'The Cabinet of Doctor Caligari' to buy a shirt and see Michael.

A moment after I walked in the door, he came steamrolling up to me. 'You cut me off! You skunk! How could you do that?'

'Cut you off? When?'

'Last night on the show! I was the one who called Rousseau. I wanted you to know I was listening.'

'That was *you*? The quote about God. Why didn't you call earlier? That was the only interesting question on the whole show. I didn't know you were such a Rousseau fan.'

He gave a satisfied grunt. 'I was going to catch the guy out with that quote from Hazlitt. The one about if mankind wished for what was right? I had it all planned out.'

'Trick him? He was just a postman from Arizona.'

'He was a fucking fake, Ingram. The other quacks on the show really believed what they were saying. Not this guy. He obviously just read *The Confessions* and decided to come on the show . . .

'Don't get me started on this. I hate fakes. Even when they're on your show.'

'I get a lot of people like that on my show, Michael. It *is* called *Off the Wall*.'

His moment-ago anger was disturbing but already gone. His face regained its softness, the 'V' of his eyebrows returned to their soft arcs. In an instant's rerun of our relationship, I realized I'd never seen him genuinely angry about anything. Why this?

'Michael, are you all right? Is something wrong?'

Instead of speaking, he took my sleeve and pulled me towards his office in the back of the store. 'I want you to see something.'

His office is small and efficient. The few pieces of furniture are grey sleek metal, and uncomfortable. The only picture on the wall is a blow-up of a still from the film *The Cabinet of Dr Caligari*, the same picture the store uses on its stationery.

'Look at this.'

He stood behind his desk and offered me a piece of folded paper. I took it and looked. There were a few words in thick red ink written on it. Very loopy, childish handwriting. The dots over the 'i's circles rather than dots – that sort of thing.

Dear Mike,

It's been a long time, right? Well, you'll be glad to hear your old pal Clinton is coming to visit you soon. So get everything for the party. I'm ready to go, baby.

I tried to hand the letter back, but Michael wouldn't take it. I put it on a corner of the desk. He looked at it unhappily.

'Clinton's coming? What's the matter with that?'

'He's already here.' Turning around, Michael pulled aside the curtain behind his desk and gestured for me to come around next to him. When I was there, he pointed across the street. His arm and hand didn't hold still. They weren't shaking, but his whole being emanated a kind of nervous, uncomfortably strong energy. As if a moment ago he'd accidentally gotten a very strong electric shock and was only slowly coming down from the kick.

29

The street was all cars and pedestrians, fumes rising, rushing sounds. Lots of people moving, moving.

'What do you want me to see?'

He jiggled a finger. 'The traffic light over there. See the boy leaning up against the pole? The one in the football jersey? Number 23?'

'The red shirt?'

'Yes. That's Clinton.'

I grinned. 'That kid is about fifteen years old, Michael.'

'I know.' He let the curtain drop.

At the last moment, 'Clinton' looked in our direction; as if he knew what was going on, knew we were talking about him.

Hands can tell you the real truth. The way they rise or fall, so often unconscious of their sadness or grace, can signal final defeat, or love that hides behind a straight face or a cynical smile.

Michael and I were sitting on opposite sides of his desk. He'd begun by trying to be funny, but his hands fluttered up only halfway – birds with no energy to rise. There was no more funny here.

'You know how many people I know, Ingram? The 'Z' section of my address book is three pages long! No lie.

'But you know what I realized not long ago? That I've always had the wrong admirers. So many of the wrong friends. Present company excepted, my greatest talent is attracting people who look great at first, but only end causing havoc.

'Clinton's the perfect example.'

Unconsciously, I put my hand up like a student with an eager question in class. 'Wait a minute! Michael, every Clinton story you've told me makes him sound like the dream combination of pal, protector . . . You've said ten times he saved your childhood.'

30

'That's true. He saved my childhood. But I'm not talking about that now. Listen, don't tell me you know any man unless he's revealed to you the secret prayer he mutters every night to his God or his devil . . .'

I shook my head uncomprehendingly: what was he talking about?

'Yes, Clinton protected me. For years. Then one day he turned into the fucking "Monkey's Paw"! The third wish that kills everything good; everything you love.'

Explaining something to someone is like sweeping the floor: first you do a series of broad sweeps with the broom to bring all the big stuff together. Then if you're thorough, you get down on your knees to catch all the little stray things that hide in the corners and far under the separate pieces of furniture. Sweep it all together and presto – a clean room.

But instead of being clear, i.e. bringing all of his Clinton Deix details together into some kind of neat (understandable) pile, Michael spoke confusingly and at times made no sense at all. His sweeping only made the dust and dirt swirl more than ever in the room that was his past.

All I really understood at the end of that first day we saw the boy across the street was this: Clinton Deix had returned and was still fifteen years old. As long as Michael had known him, Deix was fifteen.

That was over twenty years.

'I didn't tell you what happened to Anthony Fanelli.'

'Michael, please – '

'No, I'm not just going to tell you another story. This all has to do with what's happening. But you have to know the background before you can say anything. It's very involved.'

'You're telling *me*?'

Some years before, I'd had a guest on *Off the Wall* who'd been one of General Galtieri's thugs in the

Argentine government. His job had been to torture people. Although a repulsive, despicable man, particularly because he was so proud of what he'd done and pleased with having gotten away with it, he said something in the course of the show that haunted me. Most people have little pockets of learning or wisdom and he did too. His was generally predictable, but how often do we get to hear about evil from evil's own mouth? Or smell the breath of the monster, hear him discuss his trade?

What he said was this: the trick of both charm and torture is to accommodate them to your victim. You want to 'get' someone? Don't be rash, don't be too quick – find out about them, sniff around their habits and their passions. Sooner or later you'll find what you want: she likes flowers, but really *loves* orchids. Pulling out his fingernails is bad, but just mention doing something to his children and you've won; he will crawl under your foot. Charm and torture – use the same means and you can have whatever end you want. One of the other chilling things the man said was that he'd used the same methods to win his wife as he had to get information out of hundreds of doomed prisoners.

When I asked if he ever felt remorse for what he'd done, he said: 'If you pay no attention to God, he'll go away.'

Two days after I saw Clinton for the first time, the tyres on my motorcycle were slashed. That's not fun, but it's part of living in a large city one must accept. Luckily, my repair shop is only a few blocks away. I called the mechanic and we had the bike on the road again in an hour and a half. I'd moved into an apartment complex where there was a garage, but had used it only a few times. That night I did put the machine in there and thought no more about it.

Three days later my apartment was broken into. Nothing was taken, but whoever did it took shit and wrote 'Off the Wall' on my walls again and again. The smell – let's face it, human faeces has its own, very specific odour – plus the viciously intimate fact that whoever did it knew where I lived, got about five steps closer to my heart and fear. Yes, we've all read *1984* and remember the cage of rats strapped to Winston Smith's head in room 101, but that's in a book. You can put a book down and go to the kitchen for a bag of Cheese Doodles. It's different when you come home and see part of your life written in shit on your own kitchen walls.

The police saw nothing strange about it, particularly my friend Detective Dominick Scanlon who I call whenever I need a favour from the Los Angeles Police Department.

'For Christ's sake, Ingram, what do you expect with that show of yours? You got more fuckin' cranks on there than we got in jail! You're *surprised* one of them took up finger painting on your walls? Remember the talk-show guy they murdered up in Seattle? I've told you for years to watch your step. But no, you got to bring on the Charles Manson Fan Club! That show is like a living National Enquirer headline – MARILYN MONROE'S ALIVE AND LIVING IN A UFO AND CAME DOWN TO FUCK MY HAMSTER! Jesus, Ingram, are you really astonished? Only thing that surprises me is why it's taken so long for stuff this sick to happen to you.'

'Come on, Dominick, don't pull my chain. What can I do about this?'

'Move. Get another unlisted phone number. But hey, as long as you do that show, my friend, you are one radioactive dude. See, you only know those wackos when they're on your show and mostly on their best behaviour. But I see them when their reactors melt down and we got China Syndromes on our hands. Like when these guys blow their brains out, or whoever's nearest. I like you a lot, man, but you can't expect to get away scot-free when you're handling all that radiation.'

'Cops are supposed to be reassuring, Dominick. But listening to you is like drying myself with a wet towel!'

'Hey, *you* say it every night at the beginning of your show – "The Aliens Have Landed". This time they picked your house.'

Outside, heavy drizzle floated like smoke. Michael and I watched it through his kitchen window while we drank tea and ate his good homemade brownies. He held one up and shook it at me.

'What do you think the name of the god of Lovely Little Things is? The god of brownies and Earl Grey tea? Wouldn't you like to meet him? The god of good movies, your plane leaving on time, puppies, women walking by wearing great perfume . . . I'd like to know him.

'It was Clinton who did your house, Ingram. Your tyres too, probably. I didn't tell you what happened to Anthony Fanelli.'

'Michael, please – '

Anthony Fanelli hated Michael from the first day they met. Why is it that the gifted are disturbed by the duds? Why do the failures often get such a rise out of those who have the world on a string? Michael Billa was a fat little boy who, by his own account, had a complexion like a road map from the time he was ten. He once heard an uncle say to his mother that the boy would have to be a genius to survive his looks.

'I had bad skin and a thin mouth. I was a series of doomed hormones. So you know what I did? Tried to make myself *really* amusing: I wanted to be such fun. That's not a bad idea. The world always has room for a really good clown. And for me, it worked most of the time. If I was the first to make fun of my fat or my skin and did it funnier than anyone else, then I had them all beat.

'But not Anthony. He had beautiful jet-black hair. It was always as immaculate as a geisha's. Know what else I remember about him? He kept wonderful things in his pockets. He was the first person I ever knew who had a Swiss Army knife. A gold cigarette lighter. I'm sure it wasn't gold, but *we* were impressed. I think I wanted him to like me most, but he thought I was the worst. I had as much chance getting him to like me as a dog has chasing a butterfly. That's the right analogy – I was a slobbery, miserable dog, while Anthony was a big beautiful Monarch butterfly. The only difference being, he was a butterfly with a knife.'

Fanelli was good-looking, tough, charismatic. Even girls like Eddie Devon were secretly fascinated by him and he knew it. Many of us grew up knowing an Anthony Fanelli and in retrospect they're often vaguely amusing, vaguely nostalgic souvenirs on the shelves of our memory. But back then they were real and formidable and held a kind of human magic that gave them an enchantment we yearned for.

'I could do nothing right in his eyes. Sometimes I had the feeling just the fact I was alive and existed in his vicinity made him furious. Once my mother made a cake for my birthday. Being the sap I was, I brought it to school to share with my "friends". At the time, the show *Mission Impossible* was on TV and we all watched it religiously. So when I brought the cake into the cafeteria, I said, "Everybody has to eat this fast, or else it'll self-defrost in fifteen seconds!" Anthony got a look in his eye like he wanted some, but wasn't about to take a piece of anything that was mine. He got up from the table and said "Self-defrost!" like it was the dirtiest, stupidest thing anyone ever said. And you know what? None of the cool people wanted any after he left. They all got up from the table and walked away. Only Beth Ann Gunsberg stayed and that was because she was as fat as me. There I was with this big beautiful chocolate cake in front of me and too many forks.

'Then Clinton arrived. He just appeared one day in the back of English class. When our teacher, Mrs Sellars, asked him a question, he shrugged and hunkered down in his seat. Anthony was sitting two seats away and, in typical Fanelli fashion, laughed at him. That did it. Clinton, who was about the same size, only looked at him, but you could see the stakes driving themselves into the ground and the tent going up. Right then, that moment.'

'What do you mean?'

'Their relationship. Anthony chose the site by laughing at him, Clinton got out the hammer and put in the stakes. Our tent goes here? Okay, I'll set it up.

'Mrs Sellars asked Anthony the same question. He answered it with a smile and a long look at Clinton. Deix sat in the corner looking back.

'When class was over, he walked up to Anthony and said, "You just fucked the wrong cunt, Blackie."

'Anthony had the gang around him and said, "Cunt? You say you're a cunt? How interesting!" But he didn't do anything. Even then, I think he sensed how dangerous this new guy was.

'Clinton walked up to him and said, nose to nose, "I'm going to drink you, Blackie. I'm going to squeeze the blood out of you and drink it like a cocktail. Think about that, Pretty Boy."

'Then came the egg salad in the ear and we knew Anthony had made a seriously big mistake pissing *this* guy off.

'What was almost worse for him was seeing how well Clinton and I got along! The two kids Fanelli hated most were suddenly friends, which naturally meant he

37

couldn't kick my ass any more because Clinton would find out.

'An interesting thing is, I still remember the expression on Anthony's face when he'd see me with Clinton. Know what it was? The look you see on the faces of women who are married to bad men, or drunkards; guys who beat them up sometimes. Helpless, bitter and sad.

'I was bad news, but the most pathetic kid in the school was Grace Elixhausen. That girl looked like God had taken a fly swatter to her. Everything about Grace was a disaster, but she was also a damned nice person, if you ever crossed the line of horror and embarrassment to talk to her.

'Anyway, Anthony got some girl to sneak a camera into the girls' locker-room. The story I heard later was, at Fanelli's request, this "girlfriend" of his shot a whole roll of film of Grace. That poor thing. Her life wasn't bad enough, she had to have *this* happen to her. The pictures were just awful – Grace stark naked in the shower, her bushy black hair flat down on her head, a sad, lost look on her face. Jesus, those pictures showed everything. Grace from the front, the back, bending over . . . Nothing was left to the imagination.

'One Monday I came into school and opened my locker to get my books. Glued on every possible inch of the thing were these pictures. I was so stunned both by what was there and, of course, the pictures themselves that I just stood there looking with my mouth open. Finally I heard someone say ". . . Peeping Tom!" When I turned around, there was Anthony standing behind Grace. She had this indescribable look on her face. She knew it wasn't only me who'd done this. I'm sure she knew Anthony was involved. But she probably had a secret crush on him too, which only made the whole thing worse. She handled herself beautifully, Ingram. I've rarely seen anyone as composed at a moment like that. She said "Take them down. Michael. Please get rid of them." And then just turned around and walked away. Never asked me again about them. What dignity!

'I didn't tell the story to Clinton, but someone did because he called that night and asked if it was true. I tried to avoid answering, but his voice got cold and mean. He said he wasn't going to ask again. So I told him exactly what'd happened for fear someone would have embellished it one way or the other. At least, I wanted him to have it straight.'

'What'd he say?'

Michael reached for another brownie and looked out the window. The rain was still coming down in a blue-grey mist. Clinton, Anthony, Grace, Michael . . . What did these teenagers have to do with shit on my walls and the sludge of worry building in my stomach?

'Clinton said: "That's not nice. Grace didn't need that." '

'That's all?'

Michael took a sip of tea, swallowed, shook his head. 'No, that's not all.

'Besides being chubby and having bad skin, I wasn't good in school. But the one thing I *was* good at was English. Looked forward to those classes every day. The teacher was nice and I loved to read. When mid-term examinations came around, the one I didn't have to study for was English.

'The day of the test, we were all sitting outside the exam room waiting to go in. At my school, tests were given in the cafeteria. I remember that place so well – those endlessly long tables, clanking in the kitchen, the steam from things cooking, dishwashers, the workers talking quietly. God, I can even smell the school ravioli they used to serve! Remember the smells? Canned tomato sauce. Just-washed plastic trays or formica . . .

39

School lunches. But for exams, the room became all business and we went in there scared and not hungry.

'The day of the English examination, we're all sitting outside the cafeteria at eight in the morning waiting to go in. I'm talking to Perry Cochran about the test and minding my own business. Suddenly from behind, something touches me on the left cheek. I see this look freeze on Perry's face – half smile, half uh-oh. Reaching up to touch it, I felt something hard and curved. I tried to brush it off, but it zipped away and scratched my face. Out of the corner of my eye, I saw a coat-hanger! Can you imagine? I didn't even have to look to know who did it.

'I said, "Cut it out, Anthony!"

' "Cut *what* out, Lard Ass?"

' "Just cut it out. That's not funny!"

' "I think it is, Chunkie!" '

It was uncanny how Michael was able to put the perfect tone into both of the voices – the jumpy fear of a boy telling a bully to go away; then the wise-guy smirk, I'm-about-to-make-your-life-miserable threats of an Anthony Fanelli. It made me remember my own skin-crawlings at that age in the same situations.

' "Get away from me, willya, Anthony? I never bothered you."

' "*I never bothered you*! You *alive* bothers me, Billa. The day you die I'll stop being bothered."

'Quick as a snake, he hit me across the face with the hanger. Whip! It felt cold and sharp. I don't know why he did it. I guess he just couldn't stand it any more, like a shark that smells blood and goes crazy. Even when he knew Clinton would hear.'

'Jesus Christ, Michael, I hope you hit the son of a bitch back.'

He smiled triumphantly and nodded. 'As hard as I could, right on the chin! It *almost* cold-cocked him. I think if there'd been just the slightest bit more behind

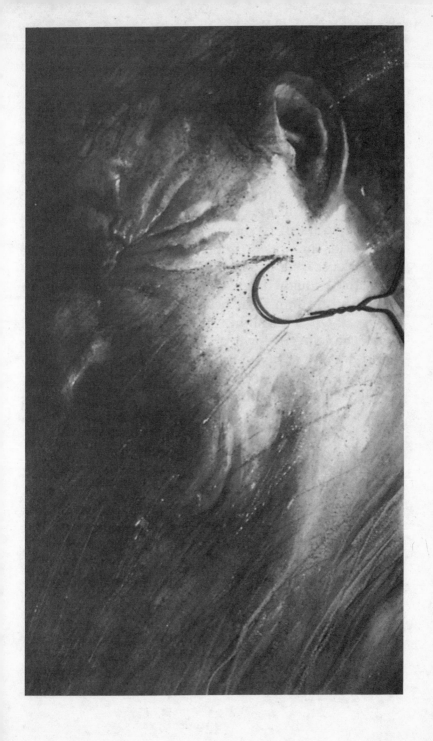

the punch it would've knocked him out. As it was, he staggered and his hands dropped. The hanger fell and made a crazy clatter on the floor. I remember *that* sound!

'I couldn't believe what I'd done. Then some girl screeched "Don't let him do that, Anthony!" And he came at me like a cruise missile. Boom!'

'Did you fight back?' I saw the whole scene and felt so sorry for the fat kid who didn't stand a chance: who'd just done the only brave act of his young life and was about to get crunched for it. I wanted him to hit back so hard; to show the Anthony Fanelli's of all our worlds he wasn't going to win just because the other was scared, or because it had always been so.

'Yeah, I fought back! As he came at me, I swung again and hit him right below the chin.'

'Great! *Good*!' I couldn't sit still in my chair. I wanted to see Fanelli go down and lose. To be shocked the world wasn't always his and was about to go away from him for the rest of his life.

Michael sighed. 'But I didn't hit him as hard this time 'cause I was so scared. He hit me two shots on either side of my face and I went down. He slipped and fell a little, trying to hit me again.

'But then this amazing thing happened, Ingram. I grabbed him and got him in a headlock! I've always had incredibly strong arms and suddenly there was Anthony Fanelli under my arm, totally helpless. But *now* what? What was I going to do? If I let him go, he'd get up and pound me. Maybe if I held tight enough he'd give up, or pass out. You know, like they always do in professional wrestling? So I just held on. It was crazy – the exam room was five feet away, any moment a teacher could have come out; but this fight had some kind of karma in it and we had to do it, no matter what.'

'What happened?'

'He punched me in the balls! So hard you can't imagine. People fought dirty then, but *that* move was taboo. You never did it. But I guess Fanelli was desperate and couldn't think of anything else.

'I've never experienced such pain in my life. I might've even passed out for a few seconds because when I came to, he was on top of me, holding my arms down with his knees. The first thing I do remember was him up there and his fist coming down on me in blurred slow motion. I don't even think I felt it hit my mouth. But I do remember my blood bursting up and splashing all over his white shirt.

' "You fuck! You fat fuck!" he kept saying over and over again as he hit me. Bap! Bap! Bap!

'Finally someone pulled him off and, like a minute or two later, we were all walking into the exam room for the test! Can you imagine? I had my handkerchief on my mouth, trying to keep the blood from getting all over me, but there was a lot.

'I sat down at my assigned seat and saw the exam paper, face-down on the desk. Remember that? Remember how the proctor'd say "Do not turn the test over until you are told"? The good old days.

'Sitting there, looking down, the first drops of blood started falling. Bloop, bloop, bloop. Right on my test. I looked at my handkerchief and saw one red mess. But there was nothing I could do, so I shifted it to a dry side and put it back against my mouth. We were told to begin. For the next few minutes I was busy trying to clear my head enough to concentrate. *And* the pain had begun. *And* I had to keep shifting the handkerchief to drier sides. Bloop, bloop, bloop.

'I was so busy trying to do all these things that, when someone sat down in the chair next to mine, I didn't pay attention.

' "Hey, what happened to you?"

'It was Clinton, who'd decided to show up for the test fifteen minutes late.

' "Nothing." I waved it away like it wasn't important. But I waved with my handkerchief and it was so full that some of the blood flew off and landed on his desk. He looked at the drops for a long time. And you know what? *I* was afraid. I knew he'd never do anything to *me*, but I was afraid, Ingram.

'Alan Piko was sitting behind us and said, "He and Anthony got in a fight and Fanelli hit him in the balls."

'Clinton asked Piko how the fight started and heard about the coat-hanger, the head lock, the punch in the balls, the punch in the mouth. Everything whispered – hiss-hiss-hiss.

' "In the balls? He hit you in the fucking *balls*?" Clinton shouted the last word and the whole cafeteria looked up. I looked down. I was out of it. I wasn't saying anything.

' "Fanelli, you greaseball shit! You hit him in the fuckin' nuts!"

'The next thing I knew, he was up out of his chair. Within a second he had it over his head and heaved the chair across the room in Anthony's direction. It hit Tom Kates instead. Kates yelled, but no one paid attention because Clinton was already running for Anthony. Think of the room in a "U" shape. We were in the middle of one of the verticals, Anthony at the top of the other. Luckily for him, because Clinton had to zig-zag to get to him. Anthony faked left and right, then blew for the door. Mrs Sellars was shouting, Clinton was shouting . . . It was bedlam.

'Anthony made it to the door a few steps ahead of Clinton. The two of them shot out of the room like Ferraris. We heard Anthony shouting in the hall "Leave me alone, Deix, you creep! Stay away from me!" His voice was loud, but had a scared falsetto in it I'd never heard before. I almost pitied him. Some kids got up and started for the door, but the teacher kept saying "Sit down and do your tests!" '

Michael took a deep breath and rolled his head as if there were a cramp in his neck.

'Did he catch him?'

He was in the middle of another neck-roll when I asked that. He stopped and looked at me. 'Yes, he caught him. Caught him and killed him.'

'*What*? What do you mean?'

'He shot him in the back. As soon as they got out of the school building, Clinton pulled out a gun and shot Anthony four times in the back and head. Then he ran away and no one ever saw him again. Except me. And now you.'

'I knew a woman who said she was in love with a man but whenever they held hands, she wouldn't take off her gloves. I knew a man who said he loved to travel to wild, dangerous places, but whenever he'd go, it was via expensive tours that guaranteed strong Jeeps and hotel rooms high enough in the tree-tops so one didn't have to worry about the warm breath of lions.'

'What are you saying?'

Mrs Blackwell looked over indignantly. She pointed her elegant nostrils at me and said, 'If you'd allow me to finish, Mr York, you would know what I'm saying in a moment.

'One must trust ghosts because they have no reason to lie. With human beings, there is always a periphery; ulterior motives abound. The dead aren't interested in promotions or a nine per cent return on their investments – '

'Ingram – ' The door opened and my producer stuck his head in. I do the interviews for prospective guests on the show and was delighted to have a break from Mrs Blackwell's pontifications.

'What's up, Arthur?'

'There's a kid outside says he has to see you. Life or death.' He shrugged.

'What does he look like?'

'About sixteen, brown hair, tall . . . Nothing special.'

'Wearing a football jersey?'

'Yes, that's him.'

I got up and went for the door. 'Where is he?'

'At reception.'

'I'll be back, Mrs Blackwell.'

What was I expecting? I had no idea. Walking along the corridor to the reception desk, I was nervous and intrigued. All the things Michael had told me about Clinton Deix were focused into one point a few feet away.

The boy sat with hands on knees, like a patient waiting in a doctor's office. The expression on his face was bored. *This* one had smeared shit on my walls? He looked more like a kid who served cheeseburgers at MacDonald's, or came to the door in a winter snow to ask if he could shovel your walk. When he saw me he jumped up and put out a hand. His face was suddenly all eagerness and warmth. 'Mr. York?'

We shook. He held on longer than I.

'Yes. You're Clinton Deix?'

'Yes, sir.'

'What do you want?' As soon as we stopped shaking hands, I crossed my arms.

'I'd like it if you'd come with me for a couple of hours.'

'That's not possible – I'm in the middle of work.'

'I know, but this is very important.'

'Why?'

'Because I know Michael Billa's been lying to you and it's dangerous if you keep believing him.'

My arms remained crossed. 'He'd probably say the same thing about you.'

Grimacing, he looked around the reception area.

46

'Can we at least go outside and talk? Please? At least do that.'

It was hot and sunny in the parking lot behind the radio station. There were only a few cars and my motorcycle there. I went over to it and climbing on, sat down. 'Did you slash my tyres?'

He shook his head. 'No! Did Michael tell you that? I didn't. That's what we've got to talk about.'

'Go on.'

There was nowhere to sit, so he squatted down with his arms around his bent knees. 'Listen, I am Clinton and I am fifteen. I'm sure he's told you that, but the whole thing's different from what he says. He's been telling you *bullshit*. He did it before, I swear to God. I swear to *God*.'

'What's bullshit?'

His arms clenched around my waist as I geared the motorcycle down and went into a curve. We were in Beverly Hills looking for an address on Walden Drive. What Clinton had told me in the parking lot had been sufficiently convincing and sinister for me to cut out of work in the middle of the day and take Deix, living time warp, onto the back of my Honda to go looking for a piece of my own past.

He said she lived on Walden Drive, was married to a rich man and had three children. Her name was Blair Dowling and she was the only woman I'd ever loved. But all that was back in high school where I spent my senior year learning, among other things, that I was gay. We'd broken up by the time graduation came around, but Blair was a witty and smart woman who I knew even then would get a good grip on the world and go on to live an intriguing life. After a few years I lost touch with her. The last thing I'd heard, she was a lawyer somewhere in New York.

47

What did Blair Dowling have to do with Clinton
Deix and Michael Billa?

'I can't tell you – you have to see and feel it for
yourself. Then I can explain it better. She's living in
Beverly Hills. She knows we're coming.'

The house was massive stone, half hidden by vines
and flowers and kitsch statues that stood watch in the
driveway. Houses like this always made me think that
whoever owned them had ripped a photo out of some
House and Garden magazine, gone to a builder and said,
'Make me this. No matter what it costs, I want to live
in this magazine house.'

I wanted to see Blair after twenty years. I wanted to
know what she had to do with Clinton Deix. When I
asked how he knew about my connection with her, the
boy told me he'd started looking for someone important
to me as soon as he knew there was a friendship blooming between Michael and me. He said he'd tried other
ways before, but none was as convincing as this.

'What has Michael done "before" that you're so
worried about, Clinton?'

He looked at me, squinting. 'He wants you to kill
me. He keeps trying to find someone to kill me because
he can't do it himself. Doesn't have the power.'

'Why not?'

'Because he's only the one who froze me. He can't
do anything else.'

I rang the doorbell. No one answered. I was about to
go away, but Clinton rang it again and said he knew
she was home. A moment later the big door opened
and there was Blair Dowling.

She looked ten pounds heavier but it made her pret-
tier. Her hair was also much shorter; the cut of a no-
nonsense, athletic woman who plays a lot of tennis at
the club and drives around with kids and big dogs in
the back of a station wagon. At first she was startled,

then seemed glad to see me. But not *that* glad, from the subsequent expressions on her face.

We all want to know what the charter members of our heart do with their lives. But the danger in finding out about them is that rarely have these significant people gone the way you expected, or the way they wanted. That's not to say their lives are failed or sad detours, but after a while of looking and listening to them recount what's happened, you know they didn't 'do' it; neither in their eyes nor yours. No matter whether they won prizes or lost all their money: what they sincerely wanted from the world, or promised themselves, just didn't happen – or worse, they weren't able to make materialize. Meet someone after half a lifetime and these signs of diminished hope or defeat are written across them like airplane vapour trails on a blue sky. Blair's life was pleasant enough, but the wealth and the kids and the love of an appealing, prominent man weren't enough. Particularly not enough for the teenage self who, I realized that day, lives on in every one of us and is too often dismayed – and then so unjustly angry – that we haven't lived up to the dreams *it* created so many years ago. Yes, our fifteen-year-old self is the harshest critic. All the things it thought we were capable of when it was in charge. All the obstacles it *knew* we'd have the power to overcome. The words 'safe' and 'cliché' would never be part of our vocabulary. We were too special, too strong. That young self was ready to be angry and thorough as a vacuum cleaner over the rest of our days.

And although we've grown to smile at (or scorn) the part of ourselves that thought bell-bottom pants were cool and we were capable of licking the world, something of that young soul lives on and watches, like a child ashamed of its parents. Only we are our own parents, our own child. No one gets left behind; every part of us sits in judgement of the other.

49

We spent an hour with Blair. After thirty minutes I wanted to leave. She had become a very genial, very capable, dull woman. If we'd met as strangers at a party, we'd have had little to say to each other. As it was, once we'd slid down the slide of our reminiscences, there was no way of climbing back up and taking the ride again. So-and-so was married, so-and-so ran a business . . . So what? These people and their lives had been important to us once, but they were meaningless now.

I suppose Blair took Clinton to be a member of my family because although pleasant enough, she said almost nothing to him the whole time we three were together. Later I realized it wasn't that so much as a talent the boy had for making himself almost invisible when he chose. It was eerie to walk into a store with him, for example, and have the sales person look at and address only me.

Although dismayed, I wasn't sorry to have met with Blair. By the time we were leaving, however, I was giving Clinton long looks, silently asking why seeing her had been so important.

At the front door after brushing cheeks goodbye, Blair put her hand on my shoulder and said, 'Ingram, I'm sorry about what happened to your friend, but I've got to tell you you *look* wonderful. It's hard to explain, but ever since you came in I've been marvelling at how alive and vital you seem. I don't have that so much. I love my family and my life, but you seem to be . . . *in* love with yours. Know what I mean? Like you're having a wonderful affair and are just beaming out all kinds of great energy. And hope! I envy you, Ingram. You're very lucky. So few people I know like their lives. They just live them and wait for what's coming next. You can't get enough of yours!'

I drove to the nearest restaurant and sat Clinton Deix

down across from me. Before I had a chance to give him the third degree, he lit a cigarette and smiled widely, at ease with the world: looking like he'd just proven everything.

'What was that all about?'

He sat forward. 'Didn't you hear what she said about how you look? It's what I've been saying! Billa found you now, when you're at your moment. It's here, *right now* you're at the top! When it happened to me, I was in high school. That fucker knows exactly when it comes to you.'

'Start again. Tell it simply, Clinton.'

I felt the weight of his frustration across the table. How could I not understand when it was so simple?

My body felt as if it were charged with electricity which made my skin tingle. What he was about to say would change everything. He put his hand in his pocket and brought out a sea shell the size of a small coin. I remember Michael saying Fanelli always carried intriguing things in his pocket when they were young.

He offered the shell to me. 'Look familiar?'

I took it, rolled it in my hand, passed it back. 'No.'

'It will. Some day soon you'll put your hand in your pocket and one of these'll be there. Maybe tomorrow, but for sure sometime soon. You'll think "Where'd I pick *this* up?" It's only a shell, so you forget about it and drop it back in your pocket. But that's when it begins; the day you find it, you're there.'

'I'm *where*? What does this have to do with meeting Blair and Michael?'

He'd ordered a glass of iced tea and took a long, thirsty swig before speaking. His cheeks sucked in over his teeth but he looked at me while he drank.

'All right, look, Michael calls it "The Essential Time". He didn't call it anything when we were kids, but now that he's an "adult" that's his word for it.

'It's like, everyone has this special time in their life

51

when they're absolutely most themselves. You know what I mean? For example, like, Hitler might've had his "essential time" when he was fifteen. Not when he was grown up and leader of Germany or anything. Maybe it was when he looked at a Jew for the first time and knew he hated him. Hated the whole fucking bunch of them.

'From what I understand, this "essential time" is when you are more *you* than at any other time in your life. A lot of people have it when they're on top. You know, like the kid in school who gets all As and is captain of this and has a great girlfriend. Everything that happens to him after is a let-down. He graduates from school Mr Hot Shit, but then ends up selling headlights or basketballs. For a year or a month, or I don't know how long, this guy . . .

'Michael always used to say it was like when you look through a pair of binoculars and have to keep adjusting them before you get a focused picture. Once in your life you're a focused picture. It comes at different times for different people, but it always comes. Sooner or later every person on earth finds a shell in their pocket. Even if they live out in the Sahara Desert or something! But no one can tell how long this moment's going to last. Michael said for some people it goes on for years, but for others it's only a short time. For some it's only a couple of *days*.'

What disturbed me most about what Clinton was saying was how closely it segued with the things I'd been thinking about Blair when we visited her half an hour before. The idea of an essential moment wasn't anything new; we all know there is a time in our lives when we shine brighter than at any other.

But that wasn't what he was talking about. What he went on to stress in example after example was how we weren't always our truest . . . selves on reaching those cherished, shining times in our lives. More often than not, the 'essential moment' comes and goes without our ever knowing it. That's why so many of us are lost and unhappy: it is our life, but we have *no idea* of its real highs and lows, the moments of real triumph or defeat, or real awareness.

Yet, like children, we are even given shells in our pockets to tell us it's here. Take advantage of your true self if you can! Do it correctly and the rest of your life will be different, profound. The only thing I can compare it to, from the things Clinton told me, is the brief moment after orgasm when we stand outside our bodies and see where we are and why we're there.

'And Michael could see this in people?'

'Not only did he see it, but he knew how to freeze them there. Like he was doing you a big favour, right? Freeze you right in the middle of your big fucking "essential moment" and let you stay there and rot for about a thousand years – '

' "Freeze" in what way?'

'How do you *think* I mean freeze, like an igloo? No! He does something and it makes you just stop. You're living and everything, but nothing more happens to your body; you don't grow no more. You don't get any older. I've been fifteen, I mean, like I've *looked* fifteen, since the day I aced Fanelli.

'Can I have another iced tea? Look, I shot that prick and then ran away. I'd been running away from my old man all my life, so it wasn't anything new. I went to New York. You can make money there if you let them do what they want to you. Then when it got cold, I'd hitch-hike down to Florida. Florida and New York were my two places, you know?

'But then I didn't grow for, like, years. My feet didn't grow and my clothes didn't get any smaller; I didn't get any taller and finally even dumb-ass me knew something was heavily wrong. I was big. I'd always been big till then, but suddenly nothing was growing any more. And my face stayed the same; I mean, I didn't ever have to shave or anything.'

The second glass of tea came and a grilled cheese I'd ordered. I was hungry but the sandwich sat there while he gulped the new drink down and wiped his mouth with the back of his hand.

'So, to make a long story short, I met this guy Larry in Port Authority Bus Terminal in New York. He looked older than me and we started talking. This was like two years after Fanelli, when I was around seventeen, I guess.'

'Didn't you ever worry about the police coming to get you for the murder?' I picked up the sandwich, looked at it, put it down.

'I was getting to that. At first I did, but then nothing happened; no cops came, no one hassled me and I sort of forgot about it, if you can believe that. But you know why no cops came? Because of Michael. He knew where I was and what I was doing the whole time. He protects you after he freezes you. That's what I call it – freezing. He might need you later for something, so he doesn't want anything to happen. You gonna eat that sandwich?'

I slid the plate over to him. 'Why should I believe anything you've said?'

'Oh, hey, I haven't said anything yet! Why should you believe? You don't have to believe nothin'. I'm just telling you for your own good.'

'What do you care about my good?'

A wise-ass smirk that looked comfortable there rose slowly over his face. 'I'm not – I'm worried about *my* own good. Let me finish this story.

'So I met this Larry in the New York bus station and we started talking. All of a sudden, he takes out this shell and asks if I have one like it. That's a pretty weird question, but I said yeah, I had one a long time.

So what? So he asks me if I know a guy named Michael Billa! Can you imagine what *that* question did to me?'

'He was one of Michael's?'

'That's right. He was one of Michael's and had come to tell me. Said he recognized me as soon as he saw me. And you know what? He wasn't lying – after Michael freezes you and you understand what the whole thing's about, you *can* recognize others.'

It was my turn to smirk. 'How come I didn't recognize you?'

Anger was all over his face in an instant. Cruel, blade-out-of-nowhere rage that was frightening to see come so quickly. He put both hands on the table as if he were about to rise.

'Look, mother fucker, don't believe any of this. But listen to me: if he freezes you, you're finished. Know what'll happen? The same thing that happened with me and Larry. Know what I did to him? Killed him. That's right. I had to do it. Know why? Michael. He wasn't even *there* and he made me do it.

'*That's* why I'm here. I don't give a shit about you, man. *I* don't wanna die. But I know you'll come for me if he freezes you. Michael only needs one at a time. When he's finished using you – or Larry, or me – he just sends his next after you and that's it.'

'Why did he need you?'

Clinton shook his head like I was the stupidest man on earth. 'Because he was one pathetic fuck as a kid. Needed a big brother, guardian angel, Gardol Shield and everything else all rolled into one. I just happened to come along at the wrrrrong time, folks.'

'Who was this Larry?'

'Michael's protector before me, when he lived in another town. You know what the guy was? His third-grade teacher!'

'Why did you kill him?'

Before Clinton answered, he reminded me of a just-

squashed cigarette in an ashtray – still lit and smould-
ering, but on its way out in a minute or two.

'I had to. Michael made me.'

I knew something was wrong almost as soon as I
opened the front door. The smells of home are both
instantly recognizable and inviolable. They change to
some degree, depending on what you've been cooking
or how recently the place was cleaned, but even onions
or new floor wax can't disguise the fragrance of your
every day; the colour we've painted the air we live in.

My first reaction was to snap my head back: the
last time the smells were different here, shit was over
everything. But once the initial shock passed, my brain
clicked in and I recognized fried olive oil, oregano,
garlic. The smells of an Italian restaurant – warm, rich
and sexy.

Since I began living alone again, I keep a hunting
knife in a vase by the front door. Not that it would do
any good if I were to go one on one with a thug, but
I liked having it there. Taking it out of its hiding place
as quietly as possible, I walked towards the kitchen.

The lights were on, the kitchen table set for one –
black place mat, white napkin, wine glass, bottle of
Chianti. Off to the side was a large earthenware bowl
filled with one of my favourite meals, 'shell salad'. The
pasta shaped like small sea shells, the kind my mother
always used when she'd make it when we were young.

That wasn't all. Moving slowly and warily through
the rest of the apartment, turning on lights, looking in
corners, I found sea shells everywhere. Three medium-
sized ones on the dresser in the bedroom. A giant
nautilus, like you hold to your ear to hear the rush of
the sea, was placed in the middle of my bed. A sign
for Shell Oil leaned up against a wall.

My apartment looked like a lunatic's shell museum.

Real ones, plastic ones, and smart jokes that made you think a while before seeing the shell in them.

For a long time that night, I moved around my small apartment hunting for the many other shells which, like an Easter egg hunt, had been cunningly hidden in strange, zany places: the tubes of the extra toilet paper in the bathroom, under my pillow, on page 1084 of the dictionary: home of the word 'shell' and its many definitions.

Without being really aware of it, I became so adept at finding them that after some time, like a good chess player, I'd stop and think, where will he move next? How can I beat him to it? And if I thought of a nice odd place to put one but nothing was there, I was pleased. How quickly we take on another's obsession.

Whoever had hidden the many, many shells must have been in there all afternoon.

Driving to work two days later, I got caught in a traffic jam that threatened to last indefinitely. One of the nice things about owning a motorcycle is, in a jam like that, you can usually weave your way in and out of cars or slide slowly along their right side to freedom. But this time even those tricks only lasted a few cars, and then I was as stuck as the rest of them.

After making sure there were no policemen around, I did a no-no: took the bike up onto the sidewalk and rode there until I reached an alley I could use to make my getaway onto a parallel street.

Extremely pleased with myself, I cruised down Detroit Street and came to a proper standstill at a stop sign; always the law-abiding citizen.

When the car passed in front of me, it took a moment to realize Blair Dowling was in the passenger's seat and that it was the same car I'd seen parked in her driveway the other day. A man was driving who I naturally assumed was her husband. He wore sunglasses and had a crewcut. I couldn't see much more, although I certainly wanted to; wanted to see the man Blair had chosen to spend the rest of her life with. The man who'd made lots of money but hadn't succeeded in making my old girlfriend happy.

Neither saw me as their anthracite-blue Mercedes passed regally by. On the back bumper was a sticker for Andover Academy.

I stayed at the intersection watching the car until it disappeared. Despite Blair's dissatisfaction, how enviably safe and balanced her life seemed at that moment. Compared to my own, it was the difference between their car and my motorcycle. One was impressive and trustworthy, albeit vaguely boring; the other *looked* wild and adventurous, but was uncomfortable for any length of time and sure didn't protect you from any of the elements.

When I got to the radio station, my producer came up to me and dropped the bomb.

'You know that kid who was here the other day looking for you? I saw him and Michael Billa last night having dinner together at Lawry's. Who is that kid, anyway? You know, that's a pretty nice restaurant, but he was in that same football jersey he wore when he came here. Doesn't he have a change of clothes?'

'*Together?* You actually saw them together? Having contact?'

'Together? Hey, Ingram, the two of them were tucking into the biggest pieces of prime rib you ever saw. And when they weren't eating, they were laughing. Looked like they were good friends.'

I pride myself on generally understanding and sympathizing with people. When you do a talk-show as strange as *Off the Wall*, you realize others' perception *isn't* often the same as your own. Also, life itself is only as orderly as it wants to be from day to day: maybe only from hour to hour.

When we read about people cutting the heads off children, or dying with a thousand others when a boat capsizes in Bangladesh, we shake our heads at the lunacy of humanity or the folly of life.

But let's face it, down deep we *know* our lives are made up of one heart-stopping near-miss after the other. There is no justice or understandable framework; there are only delays.

Sooner or later everyone hits the wall, or runs a traffic light and collides with a truck we always knew was coming. Write the word 'Cancer' or 'Pain' or 'Loss' on the side of that truck. Pray you survive the crash. That's what prayer is in the end – 'Oh God, please protect me from the inevitable.'

When the earthquake came and I pulled Glenn from the wreckage of our house and life together, one of my inner voices was as calm as sleep. It said 'So? Your time has come. It had to happen.'

But when I realized Billa and Clinton Deix were together in some kind of macabre sadistic plot against me, it was almost more difficult to absorb than Glenn's death. Death is inescapable, pain and cruelty aren't.

What did they want from me? What could I have done to deserve this kind of extraordinary planning and venomous energy? Scanlon the cop had said he wasn't surprised at the shit on my walls because of the kind of job I had. *Was* it something I'd done on *Off the Wall* that had so enraged the two of them?

And what was their relationship? Brothers? Lovers? Something even more bizarre? Where was the heart of this angry body? What had I done to make it beat so hard and fast?

My sister and brother-in-law live in Vienna. There is a nine-hour time difference which I forgot completely when I called and got a sleepy 'Hello?'

'Hi, Walker? This is Ingram.'

'Hi, Ingram! Are you okay? Is everything all right?'

In the background I heard my sister ask who it was. Their new baby began to cry.

'I have to know something, Walker. It's really very important. Remember you told me to get in touch with Michael Billa? Remember how you said we'd like each other and should get together?'

'Michael Billa? Oh yes, now I remember.'

'How do you know him, Walker? Where did you meet him?'

The line was quiet except for the long-distance hiss and whisper of nine thousand miles.

'It's a long story, Ingram. I – '

Whatever else he said was shoved aside by a loud creak in my bedroom.

'Oh *shit*!' Without thinking, I put the phone down and slowly rose from the chair.

There! Another creak.

The other place I'd lived in LA had been broken into three times. What they took doesn't matter; it's that someone has been in your home, looking, picking and choosing, feeling your life, smelling your air. When it's over, you wash every object and open all the windows.

Walking as quietly as possible to the door, I took my knife out of the vase for the second time in a week. It opened with a frighteningly loud click.

'Get out of my fucking house, Billa! Clinton! Just get out of here!'

They must have come in through the window. I was on the second floor. An easy climb up and over balcony gratings. Maybe knowing I was there . . . Maybe shouting at them would –

I turned the bedroom doorknob. As soon as I did, there was a rush of sounds inside, a flurry, a scrambling, something falling. Were they leaving? What if they had a weapon this time? What if they meant business and not just shit on the walls?

'Get out!'

A laugh inside, more stumbling. I took a breath and flung the door open.

All the lights were on. No one was there. The next thing I saw was dark red on white. Blood on my bed. But blood with other things – chunks of things. Globs and pieces . . . Meat! Big pieces of raw *meat* had been thrown onto my white bed and the blood from them was splattered everywhere across the white cotton.

'Holy Jesus!'

Thick and glistening red calves' liver. Bloody, shiny purple cow hearts, soft ivory brains like pudding. Kidneys . . .

How many pieces were there? Forty? They covered the bed. There was a gleaming pile of them in the centre.

A door in my mind slammed shut and I wasn't afraid. It was enough. It was over now. I would make it stop.

At the window I looked down. A very large dark shape was shimmying fast down a drainpipe on the side of the building. I couldn't make out who it was, but just the size alone, the fatness, said it had to be him.

'I see you, Billa! I see you, asshole!'

He laughed, but not Michael's normal laugh, deep and long. This was a child's 'hee-hee-hee'. Because of everything else that was going on, it sounded wicked and alarming.

But none of this was *funny*; nothing here had a child's laugh. It made me angrier.

I went after the son of a bitch. I went down that drainpipe so fast you would have thought I was rappeling off the side of a mountain with ropes and karabiners. Zizzzz – down the pipe, onto the ground, lose my footing, up again on the run.

The shock was how fast *he* ran. He'd touched ground

only seconds before me, but already was almost a block ahead and laughing that high awful laugh.

'You bastard!'

Hee-hee-hee.

He was too far away and it was too dark to see him clearly. But, once, he did turn around, still running, and grabbed his crotch in the old 'Screw You!' gesture. He fell down. I stopped where I was and tried to laugh. If I couldn't catch him (*why* couldn't I? How could *anyone* run that fast?) I could laugh at him, a bad imitation of his stupid kid's laugh. Hoping it would sting him a moment, wipe the victory off his face for a blink.

But he even rose quickly! On his feet again in seconds and running, laughing the same way.

I was full of the energy of outrage and wasn't going to give up until there was nothing left inside, or I was flat on the ground and finished.

We ran past warmly lit houses, people getting out of cars, trees that gave up night perfumes – magnolia, honeysuckle.

Not watching when he crossed streets, he ran a zigzag course that meant nothing to me. Was he going somewhere? Or just trying to get away anywhere?

No matter where he was going, it was plain he could have lost me if he wanted. But he ran just slowly enough now for me to be able to keep him in sight. Any moment I expected him to blast off and be gone, like the Road Runner.

When it was all gone and I had to stop, hands on knees, lungs working like bellows, I saw him standing two streets away, waiting. Was he whistling? Someone was.

I wanted to shout at him, but had barely enough energy to catch my breath.

Why did he continue to stand there in the deep

62

shadows, waiting? His laughter rose over the sound of my broken breathing.

I heard a car, something loud and powerful, come up behind me. Paying no attention, I tried to keep my eye on the enemy across the street.

The car stopped nearby. As I turned to look at it, a brilliant beam (a flashlight?) clicked on inside and lashed out across the soft dark towards Billa.

It caught him right in the face.

But it wasn't Billa. I'd never seen this man before.

'Ingram! Get in fast!'

My eyes, burnt by the light's glare, took a while to clearly see who was calling from inside the car.

Michael Billa behind the wheel. Clinton sitting next to him, the light in his hand still trained on the Meat Man. 'Hurry up! Get in or we'll never catch him!'

I looked across the street. Meat Man was gone.

'Get the fuck in the car! We can still catch up with him!'

'Catch *who*? What the hell is this?'

'Forget it. He's gone,' Michael said from inside.

'Fucking A! Will you *get* in the goddamned car, York? You messed everything else up. You think you just might be able to put your ass down in here without doing more wrong? Huh?'

Clinton threw open his door, which banged into my leg. I reached in and hauled the little shit up face to face, then slammed him back against the roof of the car. He cried out, struggled to pull away.

'Nothing doing, Clinton. Not till I hear what's going on.'

Michael grabbed me from behind. Old Tae Kwon Do lessons finally came in handy – I brought my heel down on the top of his foot without letting go of Deix. Billa yelled and fell with a fat thud beside me.

I slammed Clinton against the car again for no

63

reason other than it felt great to hit *someone* after all the shit I'd been through. No matter if it was their shit or Meat Man's, everyone but me seemed to know what was going on. Now it was time to find out and be part of the club.

Deix kneed me in the crotch.

All my breath went out in a whoosh and I bent way over to hold myself; to keep whatever was left inside inside.

'Nobody does that to me, fucker!'

'Clinton, don't!' Billa's voice.

'*Fuck* him! Nobody gets away with that!'

Something hard stuck in my neck. Even through the pain, I knew it was a gun. The hammer cocked back.

Billa screamed. 'Remember Fanelli! Clinton, Fanelli!'

'Shit.' The sound of the hammer being clicked back down. He kicked me again but hit my thigh.

Such pain I could barely stand. When I could open my eyes again, I saw Billa on his knees in front of me. So fat on his hands and knees.

After a few deep breaths I could finally say, 'What is this, Michael? What's going on? Who are you?'

He dropped his head, shook it.

Clinton was the one who said '*You*, asshole. Me and him both. Together. We're all you. You're us.'

I wasn't about to go back to my apartment, so we went to Michael's. I sat in the back seat of his car and watched the back of their heads. No one said anything.

Once there, Michael gave us beer and then got out a high school yearbook which he brought to me on the couch.

'This is Clinton. Me. And that's Anthony Fanelli.'

Typical pictures. Typical faces of American high school kids in the 1960s. The only difference was Clinton Deix looked the same in his picture then as he did today.

'I don't want to see pictures of Anthony Fanelli! I want to know what's going on! Why are you two suddenly friends? Michael, you told me Clinton was here to get me.' I looked at Deix. 'And *you* said Michael "froze" you, and wanted me to kill you!'

They looked at each other. Clinton spoke. 'Mike thought that was true. But what I said was a lie, because I couldn't tell you the truth till someone else of us understood.'

'Understood *what*?'

'Look at your palm.'

I held out my hand and turned it over. I'd had my palm read so many times on *Off the Wall* that I pretty well knew every crack and line and what they were supposed to signify. Nothing had changed there since I'd last looked.

'Yes? So?'

Both Michael and Clinton came up to me and, turning over their hands, put them down on either side of mine. The three palms were absolutely identical.

'No!'

'You can look at them with a magnifying glass and you'll see everything's the same. That's what Mike did when I showed him.'

I looked at Clinton. 'What does it mean?'

Billa answered. 'I just found out myself, Ingram. All these years, I thought Clinton had just somehow frozen at fifteen years old. Don't ask me how. Who knows what secrets life has?

'But ever since you and I met, I've been feeling stranger and stranger. Then Clinton showed up again as he has been, on and off, for years.

'I was in the shower when it came to me –' He snapped his fingers ' – like *that*. Holding this bar of yellow soap, I looked at my hand, then at my toes, and

65

wondered idly why we have *five* fingers and five toes – not more, or less. All the scientists in the world will give you logical explanations for it, but none of them are right.

'Know why? Because *God*'s giving us the biggest hint of all! The whole truth hit me there in the shower. And when it did, I walked right out, dried myself off and went looking for Clinton to ask if I was right.

'Why *does* man feel so lost or unhappy? Even when we're relatively well-off and comfortable? Philosophers have been asking those questions about life and existence throughout history.

'Wanna know why, Ingram? Wanna know one of the answers to the universe?' He smiled a little sadly and held up his hand. Showing me his familiar palm, he pointed at it.

'We have five fingers and toes because God is telling us *everything* comes in fives, even complete souls. Why does the majority of mankind feel unfulfilled in their lives? Because they're not whole. But not in the way people like Plato were talking about. All that "Hermaphroditic Whole" stuff isn't it. It's a lot simpler than that.

'Think of people as numbers. Some are ones, twos . . . But the mistake everyone makes is to think there is only *one* number one, or *one* nine hundred and sixty-two. Most societies teach us we're all individuals, if only biologically. For better or worse, there's no one else like us on the face of the earth.'

'Or ever has been!' Clinton said, shaking his head.

'Right, or ever has been. But here's the truth, Ingram, and it's why our palms are the same. There are only so many numbers. Let's say a thousand, for convenience sake.

'God makes different people, sure, but each of them has a certain number. For as long as man's been on earth, these numbers have remained the same. One to

66

a thousand. But at any one time, there are quite a few ones, quite a few twos . . .

'A complete soul, a complete number seventeen, for example, is separated by God into five parts. Each has its own important function, like the five fingers on a hand. But a hand without all its fingers is incomplete. The same is true with the soul.

'We feel lost or depressed so often in life because we go around as only one-fifth of a complete soul, floating around alone out in the world.

'The only way to be at peace is to find four other "Us"s, four other number seventeens, and come together. *That's* why God gave us that many fingers and toes. He wanted us to see them a hundred times a day to remind us of this.'

Michael sat back and let Clinton take over.

'The other day me and Mike figured out why I froze like this. Because you freeze as soon as you understand this five-part thing. I was in Florida when it came to me, but at the time I just thought it was some dumb-ass science fiction idea and didn't pay any attention to it. But it's the truth.

'You freeze the minute you understand, and don't unfreeze till you can get four others together who're the same as you to make it whole again. So since it came to Mike now, that means he'll stay frozen till we can get the others with us. You too, Ingram. Both of you'll stay like you are till the five of us're joined. Me, I stayed a teen. At least you guys got to get older!'

'But you're *telling* me this. I didn't come to any of it myself, even if I did believe you.'

Michael nodded. 'That's right, but when that first realization came, I also suddenly knew we're allowed to tell one of "us" the secret without their having to figure it out themselves. But only one. After Clinton and I spoke, we decided to choose you.'

'What's our number? 666?' I am not good at sarcasm but hoped there was some of it in what I said.

'We can't tell you that, Ingram. You'll have to discover it yourself. But you *will* in a little while, along with the other powers. Now that we've told you this, things will start changing a lot. Right, Clinton?'

The boy snorted and, blowing into his beer bottle, brought up a deep 'Toooooot!'

I looked at both of them and licked my lips before beginning. 'A complete soul is made up of five parts. Each person has a number or a shape or a colour or whatever, but only some of us realize that. Those who do have to go out looking for their, uh, complementary numbers. Right?'

They nodded.

'But if you don't ever realize this five-part thing, you go through life feeling lost?'

'Right. Ingram, I swear to God this is the truth. After two realize it and get together, they're allowed to tell *one* other who hasn't understood it yet. That's you. Now we've got to go find two others before we're complete.

'I always thought Clinton had been hexed or something and was following me around for a very bad purpose.'

'And *I* always thought Mike had hexed *me* and wanted me out of the way. That's why he made friends with you. To get me.

'But you know what we both figured out the other day? We were having dinner after Mike got it and we suddenly understood who Fanelli was!'

'One of your group? A seventeen?'

'That's right. That's why he was always picking on Mike and why I ended up killing him! We three saw something in each other that drove us nuts in different ways.'

68

'The problem is, Clinton says Fanelli was the last one of us he's seen, until now.'

'You mean me?'

Michael shook his head. 'In almost twenty years he's never seen another. Now there are three more, *including* you.'

'Who are the others?' Before either of them had a chance to speak, a thought came to me like the sound of tyres squealing before an accident. 'Meat Man!'

'Right.'

'You got it, Ace.'

'Who's the third?'

'Blair Dowling.'

'I don't believe that.'

'We knew you wouldn't. That's why you've got to see something.'

'What is it?'

'An ice cream parlour.'

I told you before Michael lived near the Larchmont section of LA, which is a part of town I've always liked. There's one wide street that's more or less the whole place, but on that street are the kind of stores you remember from when you were a child. A barber shop with a real revolving pole in front, a book and greetings card shop run by nice old women, a crowded pet store full of the familiar yip and squawk of puppies and birds for sale. We had lunch there often and went to the dime store afterward to mail our letters or just wander around and fill up on the place's 1950s feel.

There's also a small ice cream parlour in the middle of town that serves pretty good sundaes.

It was around ten thirty at night when Michael pulled up in front of this place. None of us moved.

'What am I supposed to see?'

'Just walk in, Ingram. You'll know as soon as you're there.'

69

I looked at the two of them, and they seemed to have the same expression on their faces: *any minute now you'll know what we do and it's astonishing.*

I got out of the car and took a few steps, stopped, and looked back at the car. Silence a moment, then Clinton stuck his head out of the passenger's window and said: 'All you gotta do is go in there two seconds and you'll see.'

'What if I don't see anything?'

'I'll give you a million dollars.'

I crossed the sidewalk and opened the door. A small nice tinkle from a bell greeted me. One of the girls behind the counter smiled, said, 'Good evening.'

I was about to say it back when I recognized the glow around her. Like the ecstatic moment you understand the necessary balance and magic of how to ride a two-wheel bicycle for the first time. I understood the glow around this young woman without either of us having to say anything. It was bluish and slightly shimmery, like heat waves on a summer road. There was something metallic to it, yet also a softness, as of velvet or suede.

As if to applaud my perception, she dipped her head and smiled secretly. A second later, two other familiar girls came out of the back of the store, two other identical blue auras, glows . . . whatever they were.

I stood and watched them, as if they were Egyptian princesses, exotic birds, dreams become flesh. Not that they did anything different. The first asked what I wanted. When I couldn't say anything, they looked at each other and giggled.

'Is it true?'

The first said only 'Yes'.

'Where are your others? The other two?'

'At the movies. They're off tonight.'

'But why're you *here*? There are so many other – '

'We decided that as long as we're here, we'll make

70

people happy. Ice cream parlours sell nothing but happiness.'

A family came in, the eager children rushing to the counter to peek and point at the different-coloured flavours.

'You're sure you don't want anything?'

'No . . .'

The young women turned away from me and went back to selling happiness. I walked out of the place with my mind on fire and my hands (with their five fingers) cold as ice cream.

'Now what?'

Michael was driving too fast and Clinton was lighting another cigarette.

'Now we go to Blair's house.'

'But you said she doesn't know, didn't you?'

'No, but Clinton had a very good idea that I want to try out. He thinks if we hang around her place together, perhaps our presence will push her toward knowing. It's certainly worth trying for a few days.'

'How *did* you find out about Blair?'

Clinton turned and blew smoke in my face. 'Oops, sorry! When I saw you and Mike hanging around together, I started following you and finding out who you were. Called up the station, said I was going to start a fan club for *Off the Wall* and wanted to know about you. Things like that. When they told me where you went to school and all, I got hold of a yearbook from there and saw that prom picture of you two together. Etcetera, etcetera. Simple!'

'And that's why you took me to see her the other day? Hoping we'd recognize each other that way?'

'Yeah.'

'What's her husband like?'

'A lot like you, only straight. He's made some big money.'

'But he's not . . . one of us?'

'Naah. If Blair's a seventeen, he's like an eighteen. Close, but no banana.'

'And what about the Meat Man?'

Every time I used that name, they laughed.

'He's fucking crazy, man. But the problem is, he's one of us. So now we've got to find a way to straighten him out and bring him over.'

'Why can't we just find another . . . seventeen?'

'Because it's like Michael said: I've known about this thing twenty years but've only seen the three of you in all that time. There might be a lot of seventeens around, I don't know, but the world's a goddamned big place. Like maybe there are hundreds of us in *Zanzibar* or something, but who's gonna go there to see? We got our five now. All we gotta do is round them up. Wake them up. That's why we told you in the first place. This Blair shouldn't be so hard. It's Meat Man's got me worried.'

'Walden Drive, isn't it, Clinton?'

'Walden. Right.'

'I can't get over that glow. That blue! That's what we'll look like when we're together?'

'More or less. I've only seen complete sets a few times. Once was in Talladega and they were – '

Suddenly something, *someone* big ran in front of our car in a hunch. No more than ten feet away. Stopping a moment in our headlights, she looked our way. Most shocking of all was realizing at a glance it was a woman. Maybe two hundred pounds, a snarl of a face, weirdly bright red hair. Although there was no chance of Michael hitting her, he swerved and brought the car to a jerking stop. The woman scurried away very fast. Too fast.

'Did you see the red hair, Mike? Remember that hair? Holy shit!' Clinton shouted, already throwing his door open and jumping out.

'*Eddie*? That thing was Eddie?'

''Course it was Eddie! Sure it's her, Mike! *You're* the one who told me she flipped out in twelfth grade. And we were all in school together, but we never knew! Fanelli, you, me, Eddie. Four! Already four! Oh shit, we never knew then!' Clinton furiously punched the hood of the car and took off after the grotesque hunchback.

I rolled down the window. What were they talking about? Who? The air was chokingly thick with the smell of smoke. Michael watched after Clinton, then spun and started back into the car.

'What's going on, Michael? Who was that?'

'Your Meat Man, only it's Meat *Woman*. We knew her in school. She was coming from Blair's house and your friend's got big trouble.'

'Why? Why hurt Blair?'

He cursed and spoke rapidly. 'Remember the sea-shell? That part's true. When you suddenly know, you find a shell in your pocket. But maybe the dark fifth in us always hates finding its shell. Especially our dark part! Hates discovering it's only one *piece* of the whole. We never thought someone would find out but *hate* the knowledge. And then hate the other parts too for making it that much less. Eddie Devon! Eddie Devon is going to go get all of us!'

We saw the smoke before reaching Walden Drive. Blair's house was a blooming, burning bouquet of yellow flames. Someone somewhere screamed. There was an explosion, then the crackle and hiss of what was left.

Last night, for want of something better to do, I reached into death and tickled my father. He hated it. His corpse lay in the same position it'd been in when I'd last seen him, at his funeral. So solemn. So final-looking. Eyes closed just gently enough to give the

74

feeling they might open any moment, mouth straight as a ruler line, cheeks with a blush of peach still on them.

He'd always been ticklish. You could touch him anywhere and he'd laugh. But touch his ribs and he went crazy. Even in death he jumped and his cold hands flew up, groping to stop mine. Even in death.

You can do those things when you're 'connected'. Once you're part of your whole, joined with your other four, abilities and insights come. Obviously, tickling the dead is not one of the important ones, but when I heard it was possible I had to give it a try. The others approved. We enjoyed his confusion. We enjoy anyone's confusion.

Besides, there are so few chances *to* enjoy. Who said the truth shall set you free? When Eddie Devon learned the truth about her incestuous family twenty years ago, it drove her mad. It drove her to an asylum, and to two hundred pounds, and into the kind of human being who writes with shit on another's walls. When Clinton Deix found the shell in his pocket and realized he was only a fifth of a whole, he didn't go out looking for God or his other fifths – he became a whore. He says he doesn't understand why. Eddie doesn't say anything. But we've talked about this and realized they both probably sensed something the rest of us didn't. Something that kept them from telling what they knew. Particularly Eddie. She fought so hard to keep away from us, to keep our connection from happening. Her anger and illusiveness were brilliant. I only wish now they had been more successful. She fought so hard to keep away from us, but in the end we caught her and brought her into our camp like a ferocious jungle animal hung upside down on a stick. Even after we dragged her to the ice cream parlour to show her those other five glowing so heavenly blue, she screamed and spat and did all she could to fight us from connecting with her. But we 'won'.

I remember the moment before it happened, the looks of pure triumph on our four faces – Billa, Blair, Clinton, myself. I thought, my God, we all have the same expression – what will it be like when we're *connected*? Will we glow blue too, or something altogether different? Every colour has its own beauty. I loved and envied these people their blue, but what if, once joined, our own colour transcended theirs? Flew off the end of the spectrum past white, past anything imaginable? We had spent two years waiting. Waiting for Blair's burns to heal and then for her to understand what we were about. Then working out and implementing a way to trap 'Meat Man' and force her to come in. That and other things had taken two years, but connecting took less than a second.

How we screamed! How we cried on realizing the agony of *our* truth, the hideousness of our colour. Everyone wants to go to Heaven, and everyone wants to glow heavenly blue. But truth isn't just or considerate. And there are a huge number of us who, finding our colour, are exiled in it rather than welcomed.